Hats!

Written by Dana Meachen Rau
Illustrated by Paul Harvey

Reading Advisers:

Gail Saunders-Smith, Ph.D., Reading Specialist

*Dr. Linda D. Labbo, Department of Reading Education,
College of Education, The University of Georgia*

LEVEL B

A COMPASS POINT
EARLY READER

For Charlie

A Note to Parents

As you share this book with your child, you are showing your new reader
what reading looks like and sounds like. You can read to your child any-
where—in a special area in your home, at the library, on the bus, or in the
car. Your child will associate reading with the pleasure of being with you.

This book will introduce your young reader to many of the basic con-
cepts, skills, and vocabulary necessary for successful reading. Talk through
the details in each picture before you read. Then read the book to your
child. As you read, point to each word, stopping to talk about what the
words mean and the pictures show. Your child will begin to link the sounds
of the letters with the look of the words that you and he or she read.

After your child is familiar with the story, let him or her read the story
alone. Be careful to let the young reader make mistakes and correct them on
his or her own. Be sure to praise the young reader's abilities. And, above all,
have fun.

Gail Saunders-Smith, Ph.D.
Reading Specialist

Compass Point Books
3109 West 50th Street, #115
Minneapolis, MN 55410

Visit Compass Point Books on the Internet at *www.compasspointbooks.com* or e-mail your
request to *custserv@compasspointbooks.com*

Library of Congress Cataloging-in-Publication Data

Rau, Dana Meachen, 1971–
　Hats! / by Dana Meachen Rau ; illustrated by Paul Harvey.
　　　p. cm. — (Compass Point early reader)
　Summary: A young boy tries on many different hats while trying to decide which one
to wear.
　　ISBN 0-7565-0073-7 (hardcover)
　　ISBN 0-7565-1027-9 (paperback)
　　　[1. Hats—Fiction. 2. Stories in rhyme.] I. Harvey, Paul, 1926– . ill. II. Title. III. Series.
　PZ8.3.R232 Hat 2001
　　[E]—dc21   00-011845

I need to wear a hat.

Which one?

All my hats are
so much fun.

A hat with stripes?

A hat with dots?

11

A hat with ears?

I have lots!

A hat with bows?

17

A hat with flaps?

19

Boy, I have
so many caps!

21

This hat is short.

This hat is tall.

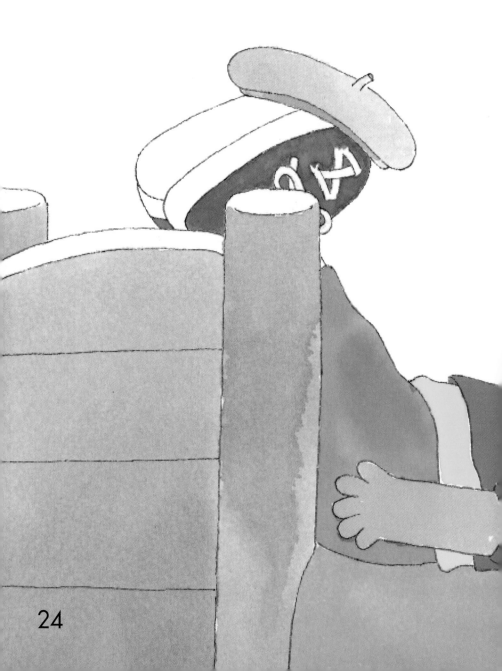

25

I cannot choose.

I'll wear them all!

29

More Fun with Hats!

You and your child can make a special and unique hat together. Have your child decorate a piece of construction paper with crayons, markers, or paint. Then roll it into a cone shape and secure it with tape or staples. Your child can glue on pom-poms, yarn, pipe cleaners, or anything else he or she can think of.

Encourage your child to see how many different hats he or she can find around the house. If he or she can't find many hats, urge your child to think of other things that could be used as hats—perhaps a cooking pot, or a box, or even an empty basket!

Word List

(In this book: 34 words)

a	hat	short
all	hats	so
are	have	stripes
bows	I	tall
boy	I'll	them
cannot	is	this
caps	lots	to
choose	many	wear
dots	much	which
ears	my	with
flaps	need	
fun	one	

About the Author

Dana Meachen Rau has many hats. When she writes stories in her home office in Farmington, Connecticut, she wears her writing hat. When she draws pictures, she wears her artist hat. When she plays with her son, she wears her mother hat. When she bakes cookies for her husband, she wears her chef hat. Sometimes, if she feels like being quiet, she wears her thinking hat. Her favorite hat of all is the warm, brown, fuzzy one she wears in winter when it is cold outside.

About the Illustrator

Paul Harvey has been illustrating children's materials for many years. He lives in Connecticut and enjoys traveling.